daal
(lentils)
daal
(lentils)

To my favorite sous-chefs:
Waleed, Musa, and Zayn, and their Abu, Kashif
—Aisha

For my family
—Anoosha

An imprint of Simon & Schuster Children's Publishing Division
1230 Avenue of the Americas, New York, New York 10020

Book design by Chloë Foglia and Tiara Iandiorio
The text for this book was set in Bitstream Cooper.
The illustrations for this book were digitally drawn.
Manufactured in China | 0319 SCP
First Edition
10 9 8 7 6 5 4 3 2 1
Library of Congress Cataloging-in-Publication Data
Names: Saeed, Aisha, author. | Syed, Anoosha, illustrator.
Title: Bilal cooks daal / Aisha Saeed ; illustrated by Anoosha Syed.
Description: First edition. | New York : Salaam Reads, [2019] | Summary: Bilal and his father invite his friends to help make
his favorite dish, daal, then all must wait patiently for it to be done.
Identifiers: LCCN 2018016711 (print) | LCCN 2018023006 (eBook) | ISBN 9781534418103 (hardcover) |
ISBN 9781534418110 (eBook)
Subjects: | CYAC: Cooking, Pakistani—Fiction. | Lentils—Fiction. | Patience—Fiction. |
Friendship—Fiction. | Pakistani Americans—Fiction.
Classification: LCC PZ7.1.S24 (eBook) | LCC PZ7.1.S24 Bil 2019 (print) | DDC [E]—dc23
LC record available at https://lccn.loc.gov/2018016711

Bilal Cooks Daal

By Aisha Saeed   Illustrated by Anoosha Syed

SALAAM
READS
NEW YORK | LONDON | TORONTO
SYDNEY | NEW DELHI

Bilal is biking outside with his friends,
when his father steps out of the house.
"Bilal, it's time to begin cooking dinner," says Abu.
Bilal's friends ask why they would need to start cooking so early.

"This dish takes patience," Abu says. "This dish takes time."
"It's the best meal of all," says Bilal. "It's . . ."

"Daal!"

"What's daal like?
Is it salty?"

"Does it taste
really good?"

"Daal is nutty and creamy
and warm like soup.
There are all different kinds.

Come see, you can help
us pick which one!"

They take off their shoes.

They wash their hands.

Bilal grabs his favorite stool.

They study the colors.

Yellow.

Orange.

Green.

Brown.

"Yellow," Elias says, "because yellow is sunflowers, rubber ducks, and the sun."

"And chana daal is my favorite!" Bilal says.

When Abu scoops out a cup of the bright yellow daal,
it clatters into the bowl.
They're small like pebbles, but shaped like pancakes.
And they slip through Bilal's fingers like sand!

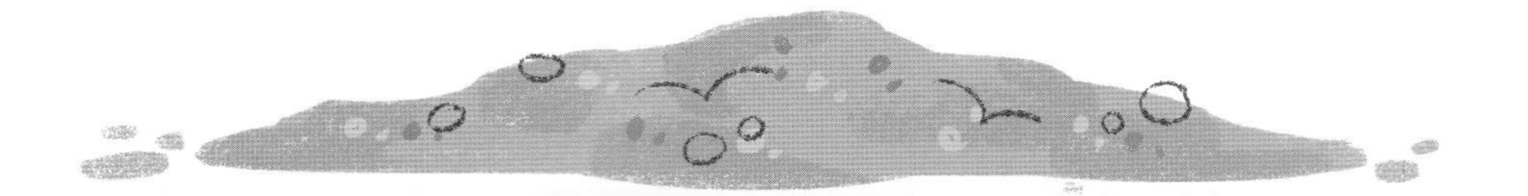

They line up the spices.
Bilal breathes in the scent of turmeric,
chili, cumin. Morgan sprinkles salt.
Elias tries to help. Bilal combines the spices.
Abu pulls out a pot, the biggest they have.

"It looks funny." Morgan frowns.
"It smells funny," whispers Elias.
"Do you think it will taste okay?"

And suddenly Bilal is a little, tiny bit worried that maybe, just maybe, his friends won't like daal at all.

"Is it ready?" asks Elias.
"Can we taste?" asks Morgan.
"No," Abu explains. "Daal takes time.
We have to wait. The flavors mix
together slowly. You kids go play
and have fun while it cooks!"

They run outside to play hopscotch. Elias numbers the sidewalk to twenty. "Let's make it longer, to one hundred," he says. "It'll definitely be done by then."

So they hop, skip, and jump to the end. Caleb and Emma join too.
"Let's check if it's ready. Let's go take a bite."

"Not yet," Bilal tells them. "Daal takes time. We have to wait."

They put on swimsuits, slip down the slide, and cannonball into Morgan's pool. Elias floats. Morgan dives. Some more neighborhood kids join them, and they all play Marco Polo.

"Is the daal done?" asks Morgan.
"It's got to be ready by now."

Splash!

Bilal squints at the sun—it's not as high in the sky.

"Almost!" he tells them. "Daal takes time. We have to wait."

They hike through the forest and skip pebbles
in the stream. The sun starts to set.
As they watch fireflies glow, they hear Abu call out,

"Bilal
It's almost time!"

They march up the cobblestone steps.
They knock on the yellow door.
And as loud as they can, they ask:

"IS IT DONE?"

"Come see." Abu smiles
and opens the door wider.
The kids rush inside.

Bilal lifts up the lid. He peeks in the pot.
Abu says, “Ready for the final steps!”

They dice up the onions,
chop ginger,

press garlic, squeeze lemons, and top it off with fresh cilantro.

Bilal puts out plates.
Abu sets out the naan. The kids
pull up every chair in the house.

Bilal watches his friends take
a spoonful of daal. . . .
"It's steamy," says Morgan.
"Like soup!" says Elias.

"It tastes garlicky
and salty and sweet."
"I like the onions."
"I like the lemon."

"And the way it's so creamy,
it melts in your mouth!"
"Daal takes time. We had to wait, but,
Bilal, you were right—daal tastes great!"

Bilal looks at his dad and smiles.
Abu winks. “Tasty, isn’t it?” he says.
“Like my Ammi once made. My friends
and I helped her once, like you.”

Daal is tiny. Daal is tough. But with a little time, and a lot of patience, it becomes the softest, tastiest, best thing in the whole wide world. And the best part is sharing it with friends.

That's why Bilal loves daal so much.

Author's Note

Daal is a staple food in much of South Asia, including in Pakistan, where Bilal's grandparents grew up. Daal, also known as lentils in English, is the name of a thick vegetarian stew full of healthy protein and vitamins. There are many different types of daals, each with their own color, shape, and flavor. Some cook quickly, and some can take all day to make just right. People eat daal with rice, bread, and sometimes just with a spoon.

Chana Daal Recipe

(Please ask a grown-up for help.)

Ingredients

1 cup chana daal
3 cups water
1 tablespoon turmeric
1 teaspoon salt
1 teaspoon chili powder
1 teaspoon cumin powder
1 teaspoon coriander seeds
3 tablespoon olive oil
1 diced medium onion
1 sliced jalapeño (optional)
1 teaspoon minced ginger
1 teaspoon minced garlic
1 diced medium tomato
1 teaspoon lemon juice
1 tablespoon garam masala
3 tablespoon fresh cilantro (optional)

Directions

Rinse and drain the chana daal.
Place daal in slow cooker.
Mix water, turmeric, salt, chili powder, cumin powder, and coriander seeds into the pot.
Cook on low for 8–10 hours or on high for 4–5 hours.
In a frying pan, add oil and fry onions, jalapeño, ginger, garlic, and tomatoes together and cook until softened (7–8 minutes).
Mix the sautéed vegetables into the slow cooker, add lemon juice and garam masala and stir.
Top with fresh cilantro for garnish.

daal
(lentils)
daal
(lentils)